Once he found himself alone in the dark, so full of mystery, with each tree seeming to conceal a trap, Agouhanna felt paralyzed. He breathed with difficulty and his heart was leaping in his breast. How would he be able to dive into the woods, into this unknown? . . .

The forest was filled with suspicious sounds. Even though he could still see the high wall of the village, Agouhanna could not endure it. He started at the slightest alarm, ready to flee. He was so desperately anxious for the arrival of the reassuring daylight!

All of a sudden he heard a muffled, rhythmic sound. It had to be some large animal, for the dry branches were cracking and breaking under its heavy steps . . . A bear! Yes, Agouhanna couldn't be mistaken, it was surely a bear.

AGOUHANNA

AGOUHANNA

BY CLAUDE AUBRY

TRANSLATED FROM THE FRENCH BY

HARVEY SWADOS

ILLUSTRATED BY JULIE BRINCKLOE

PaperJacks

A division of General Publishing Co. Limited
Don Mills, Ontario

Published in PaperJacks 1973
Reprinted by arrangement with
Doubleday Canada Limited.

ISBN 0-7737-7051-8
Printed in Canada

AGOUHANNA

It was just before the coming of the white man. Among the Indian nations which people North America, the Iroquois had become very powerful. They had a reputation far and wide for being proud, fierce, and dreaded warriors. Feared like the plague, they learned the violent profession of the warrior from earliest childhood.

At this time, in a village stronghold situated on the banks of Lake Huron, there lived an Iroquois chieftain known as Black Eagle. He had been a great commander. A warrior since the age of fifteen, he had fought bravely all his life against the enemies of the Iroquois.

Now that he was old, he fought no more. Everyone venerated him, but he never spoke a word to anyone, not even to his own wife, who was still youthful and high-spirited. No one could recall ever having seen him smile, not once. A great sorrow troubled him, and the entire village suffered with him: He did not have a son to succeed him as commander and chieftain of the tribe.

One morning, it appeared to everyone that Black Eagle had gone mad. Casting off his customary dignity, the chief ran, laughing and gesticulating, from one hut to the next. In the eyes of the villagers he seemed possessed by an evil spirit. They were already weeping for him, when the extraordinary news swept the village like a stray arrow—a son had just been born to Black Eagle.

This birth had been welcomed as a benefaction of the Great Manitou, the god of the Indians, and greeted with huge festivals which went on for many days with banquets, dances, games, and songs. The child was named Agouhanna (which means "brave among the braves" in Iroquois). He had to bear this name until the age when he would become a warrior. According to Iroquois custom, a boy changed his name when he became a warrior.

Like all the other little boys of the village, Agouhanna spent all his time with his mother until he was six years old. During the winter he played in his parents' large cabin. He loved to watch his father smoke his pipe, or carve animals out of maple logs. He felt a joyous hunger come upon him when he saw his mother toss splendid ears of golden bantam corn and succulent morsels of dried fish into the large stewpot hung above the fire from which there drifted, in a gentle blue haze, the pleasant and promising odors of a good boiled dinner. All of this made him very happy, even if now and then he felt suffocated by the thick smoke coming from the fire in the middle of the room, which filled the cabin. There was indeed an opening in the roof to allow the smoke to escape, but often, because of the winter winds and the humidity, a substantial portion of the smoke didn't get out, and spread throughout their dwelling, irritating his throat and his eyes.

But Agouhanna got used to that. For him as for the other Indian children, the winter passed. Then came springtime, rather disagreeable. And finally summer!

Summer was the beautiful and hot season. Young Agouhanna played in front of the doorway, while his mother stretched reindeer and wolf skins to dry them out. From these hides she would make blankets for their pine needle beds, clothing, and shoes. Agouhanna would go with his mother to the brook where she drew out a fine, clear, cold water in pails made of bark.

He also went into the woods and the neighboring glades with his mother, and helped her to pick strawberries and raspberries, plums, and wild grapes. They filled their bark buckets and woven baskets to the brim. Sometimes they came back late in the evening, after sundown. Terrified by the darkness and the mysterious sounds coming from the depths of the forest, the little Iroquois pressed against his mother, trembling with fear.

His mother pretended that she noticed nothing, and didn't speak of it to the old chieftain. Once at home, she served the soup that simmered in the pot, then put Agouhanna to bed on his fine bearskin and rocked him to sleep, singing the song of the moon and the stars to him.

With his mother, he also went to fetch the dead wood that they stacked up by the cabin to feed the fire during the long, very cold winter months. He could remain motionless for long hours, watching his mother play with mud— suddenly, to his great surprise and his great joy, he saw jars and plates of all shapes emerging from his mother's hands. He clapped, believing that his mother had magical hands. She glanced at him sideways, then smiled at him without saying a word. After drying out her pottery, she

decorated the pieces with pleasing and mysterious designs.

That was the way Agouhanna lived until he was six years old. Until then he had been neither better nor worse than the other little Iroquois of his age. But starting from that period things began to get spoiled for Agouhanna. This is why: When a little Iroquois reached the age of six, he had to undergo his first trial. There was no way out of it; he simply had to endure it. No exception was made for anyone. That was the custom.

Here is what the ordeal consisted of: The father made a miniature bow and some tiny arrows for his son, and then taught him how to use them. After that, these little Iroquois would be brought together very early in the morning, taken to the outer side of the great gate of the stockade that surrounded the village, and left to wander in the neighboring forest where they had to hunt for small game (birds, squirrels, hares, etc.). They were warned not to go too far away, and always to manage to stay near enough to hear the voices coming from inside the fort. In that way, the songs coming from the fort would guide and support them.

Like the other fathers, the old chieftain had spent long hours secretly and lovingly making a bow for his son. It was the finest bow one could find, decorated with birds, flowers, and feathers. The old chieftain was terribly anxious for Agouhanna to reach the age to make use of it.

A little before Agouhanna turned six, his father brought forth from their hiding place the fine bow and the arrows neatly arranged in a little leather quiver adorned with warrior designs. He hung the quiver from his son's shoulder, placed the bow between his fine delicate hands, then stepped back a bit to see what a splendid warrior his son would make. To his father's great surprise, Agouhanna displayed no joy at this gift. His expression was, rather, frowning and thoughtful.

Very early one morning all the little novice hunters, including Agouhanna, were assembled with great pomp in the village square. Each one was armed with his bow, and little arrows exceeding the capacity of their quivers. Already you could see the resolute expressions on their would-be-tough little children's faces. Their fathers—and the older brothers of those who were orphans—stayed near them.

In his capacity as commander, Agouhanna's

father gave the signal for the departure. The little hunters, with Agouhanna in the lead, headed for the path leading out of the village. Fathers, mothers, sisters, brothers, accompanied them to the great gate of the stockade where they stopped, leaving the children to cross by themselves the threshold of this great doorway which led out into the forest.

Until then everything had gone off very well. But once outside the high wall of the village, and facing for the first time the dark and mysterious forest without their mothers, the little hunters broke off their forward rush, even stopped still, crowded into a cluster like a swarm of bees, hestitated for a moment, then plunged one by one into the forest.

Inside the walls, the crowd sang a rhythmic chant in unison and without pause in order to guide the young hunters, to prevent them from going too far away, and to indicate to them on their return the whereabouts of the village.

The little Iroquois ran off in all directions, silent as fish in a stream so as not to frighten off the game. Agouhanna advanced several paces among the huge trees, but as his companions were already far off and he found himself alone before this dark and mysterious monster that the forest was to him, he froze, nailed to the ground by fear. He turned his head and looked back at the high wall some five hundred feet behind him. The heavy gate had remained open, in order to greet the first happy hunter who would return eagerly and proudly with his first trophy, thus winning the prize that would be awarded to him by the chief. But when he thought of the pain and the shame that this would bring to the old commander, he didn't dare to retrace his steps.

Agouhanna remained like this for a long time, standing in the tall grass without budging. Suddenly he heard a slight sound right next to him. Before he could utter a word, his friend White Eagle stepped before him, holding a bloody hare by the ears.

"What are you doing here?" whispered White Eagle in astonishment.

Agouhanna looked at his friend's hare and all but vomited. The sight of that blood horrified him. He lowered his head without uttering a word.

"Why aren't you hunting with us?"

Agouhanna kept his head down and remained silent for what seemed a long while, then began to cry. He was afraid, and he was ashamed of being afraid.

"I'm afraid," he finally confessed to his friend. "I'm afraid, all alone in the forest, and I can't help it."

And he trembled all over. White Eagle couldn't keep from casting a scornful glance at the old chieftain's son; then after a moment, he relented. "Come on, take this hare and run back with it to your father!"

Agouhanna began to protest sharply. "What about you? You were skilled and brave, since you're the first to come back with a head of game. So you're the one who should have both the honor of arriving first and the reward of the chieftain."

"Nonsense! I couldn't care less about rewards. My pleasure would be far less than your father's disappointment. You go bring him this head. Wait! Throw away an arrow from your quiver and take this one here, it's smeared with blood. Then your father will surely believe that it's you who made the kill."

Without a word, Agouhanna took the hare that his friend held out to him and began to run toward the village gate. The chief, seeing that it was his son who was racing in first to receive the prize, received him with tears in his eyes. All the women surrounded him and embraced him, congratulating him on his exploit. Only Agouhanna did not show a great deal of enthusiasm, receiving the praise with lowered head and eyes on the ground.

Believing that he was behaving like this only

because of modesty and refinement, everyone praised him all the more. Later in the day, many others came back with cries of joy, triumphantly waving here a squirrel, there a swallow, there a hare. And the others? Alas! They returned in chagrin, empty-handed, heads low. Would they become real warriors someday? It would certainly be necessary for them to do better at their next test.

They closed the great gate of the stockade once again and began the celebration for the young hunters. Everybody—men, women, and children of the village—gathered in the main square. The young conquerors formed a solid circle in the middle of the square. They danced and danced to the rhythm of the drums and hunting songs. At the end of each turn, a beautifully colored, glittering necklace was slipped over their heads, after which the dance began again with renewed ardor. During this time, according to custom, the game was cooked and cut into little bits which were distributed to everyone present as a way of showing that the young boy was already a man capable of supplying the provisions for his own people.

When the moment came to award the winner, they had Agouhanna step up to the group of elders, in the middle of whom stood the old commander. As he bowed toward his father in order that a magnificent crown of feathers could be adjusted on his head, Agouhanna noticed White Eagle, who was watching him, seated in the middle of the group of unlucky hunters. At that moment Agouhanna felt himself melting with shame. This coronet on his head should really be presented to White Eagle. How White Eagle must despise him! And his father—how his joy and pride would turn to shame if he knew the truth! No, he could go on playing this game no longer.

At the very instant that he was going to dart toward White Eagle to take him by the hand and lead him before the elders and shout forth the truth before everyone, he felt the crown settle gently on his head, and the long hands of his father brush his cheeks. He did not have the strength to stir, nailed into place by this gesture of his father and the applause of the crowd.

From this day on, the young hunters could wander off at will from home, and even upon occasion venture farther and farther into the forest. Before, they had been under their mothers' protection, but now they were free little men. They were all delighted with this, all except for Agouhanna, who couldn't resign himself to being separated from his family.

The village understood nothing of this. Agouhanna himself knew: It was fear that kept him

near his mother. He could not behave like his little comrades, and he suffered from it. He even envied those who walked around in front of their parents' cabins, faces blackened with charcoal by their mothers, who had punished them in this way for some misbehavior. And this despite the fact that the poor scamps couldn't go inside their homes, or eat, as long as their faces were black. At least, they had had the courage and the pluck to commit mischief. He himself, he knew, would not have been able to bring himself to misbehave—nor his mother to punish him.

Two years passed in this way, and Agouhanna still could not bring himself to leave his mother's skirts. She did not complain, preferring to keep him close to her; but his father began to be seriously disturbed.

One spring day, while Agouhanna was helping his mother to stretch some beaver skins in front of his parents' cabin in order to have them dry in the sun, he saw a group of boys of his age coming toward him. They were uttering loud

cries and waving their bows and little shields.
They stopped before Agouhanna.

"Are you going to play war with us?" asked
White Eagle. "You'll be our new chief."

The invitation gave him real pleasure, and the
gesture was just like his friend, but at the
moment when he was going to accept, with a
joyous leap full of gratitude, one of the boys, the
son of the old witch doctor, spat on the ground
and muttered contemptuously, "Agouhanna
will never be able to become a warrior, because
he's always hanging onto his mother's skirts.
He's a girl, and his mother is going to show him
how to make moccasins and scrub out cald-
rons."

All of the boys except White Eagle began to
laugh loudly, for among the Iroquois only
women do such tasks, and mothers teach them
to their daughters from earliest childhood. Then
they all spat at Agouhanna's feet as a token of
contempt. White Eagle threw a despairing
glance toward his friend, whom he could not
defend without affronting him. It's lucky, he
thought, that Agouhanna's mother isn't here, or
his father either, for that would have been the
last straw! He really did wish that his friend
would throw himself on the witch doctor's son.

Agouhanna himself was suffering from it, and
burning to throw himself on the insolent boy,

but was paralyzed by the fear of being struck. He looked at the little group as if he were going to weep, turned on his heel, and vanished into the cabin at a run. He threw himself flat on his face onto his bearskin, held his head in his hands, and began to sob.

He wept for a long time, and eventually cried himself to sleep. When he awoke, his mother was on her knees beside the bearskin and was caressing his hair. She asked him gently what was wrong. Agouhanna gazed at his mother as if this were what he wanted, then in a sudden bound pressed himself against her, but without uttering a word. At this, his mother began to sing a long slow chant, rocking back and forth, and the child calmed down, then fell asleep once again. His mother covered him with a warm beaver robe.

The time had come for the second ordeal. Inevitably, Agouhanna had to participate in it along with all the other young boys of his age. All those who emerged victorious would become real hunters. From that day forward they would be free to go and hunt when and

where they wanted, without even asking their parents for approval.

This is what the new ordeal consisted of: Carrying nothing with him but a bow and some arrows, the child had to spend three whole days alone in the forest, sleeping under the stars, and eating whatever he himself could catch. Those who, driven by hunger or fear, returned before the end of the third day, would still be considered as children. The others would become adults.

Naturally, Agouhanna did not look favorably on this trial. The youthful participants were frisking about impatiently. They were in a tremendous hurry to reach that long-desired moment when they would be allowed to come and go freely, as they saw fit, in the forest.

Agouhanna knew that fear would grip him as soon as he found himself alone in the forest. But he could not refuse to undergo the trial—the scandal would have been too great. He would be pointed at. They would never accept him as a successor to his father, who was considered a hero. Worse still, his father would die of shame. Yet he could not get used to the idea of spending three days and—what was worse—three nights alone in the forest, in the midst of bears and wolves. To say nothing of the fact that some enemy warrior might be able to surprise him and strike him down with a hatchet blow, or take him prisoner in his tribe in order to make him a slave.

When he lay stretched out on his bearskin at night with his eyes wide open and thought about everything that might happen to him, a cold sweat broke out over his entire body and made him shiver. It was simply out of the question for him to go out alone into the forest—he'd die of fear! How could he get out of this terrible situation? If only he could find a way!

By dint of thinking hard, he came upon a way which would certainly be humiliating for him, but which might save him. It was this: he would go see his friend White Eagle and ask him to keep him company during their stay in the forest. They would spend the time of their ordeal together.

"White Eagle, I have a plan."

"A plan? For what?"

"For our next trial."

White Eagle flexed his bow and skillfully shot an arrow which lodged in the trunk of a young birch tree. It whistled in flight, and, when it had impaled itself in the heart of the tree, vibrated for some seconds before resting motionless. During all this time, White Eagle kept his eye on the arrow. Then he turned back to his friend, who had been admiring the shot, and said to

Agouhanna

him, throwing him a glance from beneath his lids, as if he guessed what his friend was going to propose to him: "What is your plan?"

"As you know, in the next test each of us will have to stay alone in the forest for three days and three nights."

"So?"

Agouhanna lowered his head and mumbled very softly, humiliated, "I don't want to stay alone in the forest, especially at night. I think I'd die from it. You just have to help me."

Annoyed by his friend, White Eagle turned his head and looked away. "How do you suppose I could help you?"

"By keeping me company in the forest."

"You're crazy! If they saw us together, that would mean dishonor for both of us. We'd never be accepted after that, either as hunters or warriors."

"I've already told you that I have a plan. Now listen: We'll leave, each of us in his own direction; then we'll meet at a certain point in the forest, not too far from here. We'll spend the three days together hunting, then each of us will come back to the village by a different path with the spoils of our hunting. But you're the one who will hunt, because as you know I don't like to kill animals."

"How can you talk like that when someday

20

you'll become the chieftain of our village and the commander of our warriors?"

"I won't be either the chieftain of the hunters or the commander of the warriors, but rather the leader of those who love animals and will not kill them."

"How will you be able to feed your village, if you don't want anyone to kill animals in order to eat them?"

"I haven't thought about that. It's true, it's a problem. I no longer know what I'd do . . . At any rate, I do know that for myself I wouldn't be able to kill any."

"I don't understand you, Agouhanna, or your girlish feelings, being afraid of blood and all that —but I like you a lot, and you do talk admirably. Maybe at bottom you're the one who's right. After all, haven't you been like a brother to me? So I accept, and I'll do what you want."

"Thank you, White Eagle, you're saving my life."

"Just the same, to be fearful at this point! And to be the son of a great and courageous commander! I still don't understand."

And White Eagle shook his head with a very sad expression. Wild with delight, Agouhanna began to laugh at his friend's attitude, and, suddenly feeling both brave and confident, jumped on his companion and tugged at his hair, then escaped with the grace of a gazelle. Without quite knowing where he was heading, he ran full speed until, all of a sudden, he found himself in front of Little Doe.

Seated on a log before the door of her cabin, she was shelling corn kernels for her mother. Agouhanna stopped, all out of breath. He looked at the little girl and smiled at her. He thought Little Doe was really pretty, and her stubborn expression amused him. Perhaps his footsteps had led him to her without his even being aware of it. He felt happy, and he wanted to say so to Little Doe. He loved Little Doe that much. To tell the truth, aside from his father and mother, she was the one whom he loved more than anyone else in the village, more than even White Eagle, his very best friend!

At this thought, Agouhanna turned around to see if his friend was still chasing after him. But doubtless White Eagle had sized up the situation at a glance and had hastened to get out of sight. Agouhanna looked all around him—not a soul. Perfect! Little Doe's mother was used to seeing a good deal of him with her daughter. But the others in the village, especially those of his age, would at once have taken him for a little girl, as certain people already had a tendency to do, since boys were supposed to scorn and ignore girls. Embarrassed and anxious to regain his confidence, he said to her, "You know, we're leaving for the hunt in three days."

Little Doe had stopped working when Agouhanna had come running into view. She, too, liked the young prince. His manner was so refined, so kind, so affectionate and sensitive! She let herself fall into a daydream that someday he would become her husband. Then she drove the dream away, since he would doubtless marry the daughter of another chieftain. That was all the more likely because her father was only a humble warrior who had allowed himself to be captured by the Hurons who held him prisoner, enslaved. In spite of that, she loved her father very much and thought of him often. Even if her mother was contemptuous of him because he had let himself be taken by enemies, Little Doe secretly preferred knowing that her father was a living prisoner rather than a dead hero. She felt that she herself would never have behaved like that, but she didn't want to judge her father. She raised her eyes and cast an admiring glance at Agouhanna.

"How brave you all are, you boys!"

"Oh, go on!"

Before Little Doe's frank and clear gaze Agouhanna suddenly felt ashamed. It was as if all his joy had fled. He became gloomy and thoughtful. To keep himself in countenance, he picked up a fistful of corn kernels from the big bark platter and tossed them into the air. Then he ran off, his ears ringing with the indignant cries of Little Doe, who shouted abuses after him, calling him a loafer and a washout as a hunter.

Even if she had to share the inferior status imposed on girls by the traditions of her people, her sarcastic disposition and her forcefulness made her redoubtable, and the young boys of her age feared and respected her. Like those boys, she was lazy, and already she detested the chores that the tribe relegated to women. On the other hand, she loved to hunt and knew how to handle the bow like a true warrior.

She devoted herself to it in secret, since she didn't have the right—or at least, people wouldn't have looked on it favorably; but the whole village was aware of her skill. They pretended to ignore it, thinking no doubt that it would all pass with maturity. Among the Indians, children were kings, and people respected their whims. They did practically anything they wanted to, and were rarely punished.

Little Doe followed Agouhanna with her eyes as he zigzagged away from her, skipping about like a butterfly. Then she began to laugh, and her anger was blended with a great tenderness. Agouhanna was so different from the others!

She gave a long sigh. Looking at the pile of corn ears she had yet to shuck, she made a face—there was still enough to keep her busy for hours.

❉

Once he had made the arrangements with White Eagle, Agouhanna felt calm and confident. He no longer felt afraid. He even made a show of a certain impatience, and started to count the days until the beginning of the long hunting trip in the forest.

Finally the day of the ordeal began. Like all the other young hunters, Agouhanna was awakened very early. Calmly he donned his very finest garments. The commander observed his son stealthily and could not keep from admiring his coolness and composure. When his son was ready, he handed him a quiver adorned with embroidery and filled with arrows. The boy had to adjust it on his shoulder himself. His father also gave him a bow larger than the first one. His mother tried to slip a slice of smoked venison swiftly under his clothing, but a stern glance from the chieftain halted her gesture. With her lead lowered, she put the meat back into its storage place. Agouhanna thanked her with a smile, saluted his father, and left.

It was still very dark, and the boy could hardly discern the other cabins of the village. Shaking and shivering, he headed toward the path out of the village. Finally he made out a dark and vaguely stirring mass near the great gate—the young hunters. He had scarcely rejoined his comrades when two warriors of the village opened the great massive gate, made of thick logs and posts. Through the gap in the open gate the forest loomed, black and menacing. At the sight, the little group of children involuntarily recoiled, hesitating. This time was not like the first, when the entire village had accompanied the troop of young hunters, parading with them right up to the exit, with embraces and with songs that would give them their bearings toward the fortress.

Now came the real initiation to the hunter's life in the woods. It was stern and serious. Not even the chieftain was there to salute their departure. All the youngsters wore anxious expressions. The entire setting moved them deeply—which was just what was desired.

At last, they ventured forth. As soon as they were outside the wall, they split up, each one taking a different path.

Once he found himself alone in the dark, so

full of mystery, with each tree seeming to conceal a trap, Agouhanna felt paralyzed. He breathed with difficulty and his heart was leaping in his breast. How would he be able to dive into the woods, into this unknown? He wanted to cry out, to call out for help to his mother, to White Eagle, even to his father. He took several steps at random, then slipped under the shelter of a huge pine tree and awaited the daybreak.

The forest was filled with suspicious sounds. Even though he could still see the high wall of the village, Agouhanna could not endure it. He started at the slightest alarm, ready to flee. He was so desperately anxious for the arrival of the reassuring daylight!

All of a sudden he heard a muffled, rhythmic sound. It had to be some large animal, for the dry branches were cracking and breaking under its heavy steps . . . A bear! Yes, Agouhanna couldn't be mistaken, it was surely a bear.

The slow and regular steps drew nearer. Agouhanna was seized with panic, and came close to fleeing at top speed. But his legs were leaden and he could not budge. Suddenly, Agouhanna saw the dark massive silhouette of a bear take form, emerging from the dimness. The beast went straight toward the little Iroquois. It approached close enough to touch the pine tree with its snout. Agouhanna came near fainting.

Despite his terror, he succeeded in holding his breath for more than a minute, without moving a muscle, as if he had been carved from wood. The bear rubbed his damp muzzle three or four times against the rough pine branches, uttered a rumbling growl that made Agouhanna's hair stand on end, turned around slowly, and disappeared as he had come.

Agouhanna was finally able to breathe steadily. The blood was pounding in his head like the roar of the sea.

Little by little, he could see a tiny shaft of light broadening among the trees—daybreak was coming at last. Never had the young Iroquois welcomed the arrival of a new day with such delight: He greeted the singing of the birds with a glow of thankfulness. No longer was he in the mysterious realm of the night, in which so many dangerous creatures moved about. The birds were his friends. He loved their song above all. Listening to them, he felt himself surrounded by peace and security.

Encouraged by the brightness of the day and the singing of his friends, Agouhanna set off to rejoin White Eagle at their agreed-upon place. Since his clothes were soaked by the morning dew, he paused for rather a long time in sunny spots to give them a chance to dry. When the sun's warmth had penetrated him, he felt strong, confident, and happy. So he began to sing too, making up some very fine songs as he went along.

Agouhanna walked for a very long time. By now the sun was directly overhead, in a cloudless blue sky—but there was still no sign of White Eagle. By the time they were old enough for this second ordeal, the young hunters knew the forest well for miles around. But Agouhanna was unable to locate the spot where he was supposed to meet his friend. No doubt he had taken the wrong path at some particular moment. Hunger pangs began to gnaw at him. Nevertheless he continued on his course in the hope of finding his friend before darkness fell.

Then he reached a spot that resembled the one of their rendezvous. But White Eagle was not there. Just the same, Agouhanna stopped there—he didn't want to venture any farther. Still hoping that his friend might rejoin him, he made himself a bed of moss and stretched out on his back, diverting himself by looking up at the sun's rays that pierced through the leaves of the trees like long, glowing shafts. To appease his hunger he chewed on some bitterroot.

Many hours passed in this way, and White Eagle still did not show up. Suddenly Agouhanna could no longer see the gleaming shafts of sunlight. So he clambered up a large tree and

watched the sun slowly disappear behind a mountain. Below, all around him, the forest grew darker and darker.

Agouhanna came down from the tree. He began to be very afraid. Suppose he had to spend another night alone in the forest, this time far from his friends? He trembled, and felt his legs grow weak. Surely something had happened to White Eagle! Now what should he do? Plunge deeper into the woods in the hope of finding White Eagle? Of course not, that was out of the question. He'd die of fear. Return at once to the village? He'd be the laughingstock of the village—and what a humiliation for his father!

Come on! He simply had to think of something, and fast, before it grew too dark . . . He had it! Suppose he wounded himself with one of his arrows? He'd be able to return to the village, and they'd think he had had an accident.

Agouhanna drew an arrow from his handsome quiver and pressed the point of it against the firm brown flesh of his left arm, near the shoulder. But he couldn't bring himself to push it into his arm. At the thought of the blood that would spurt out, he all but fainted. Throwing the arrow far from him, the boy flung himself on the ground, buried his head between his folded arms, and began to sob. He felt so completely alone and abandoned! His entire body shook and shivered.

Suddenly, a branch broke with a dry crack. Silence, then a slow, heavy step. The little Iroquois thought that it was the bear that he had glimpsed in the morning. Arising with a leap, he started to run as fast as he could in the direction of the village. He had only one idea in mind— to reach the village before nightfall. If he went quickly enough, he would get there. You would have said that he was borne on wings. His feet barely touched the ground.

He ran for a long time like that without stopping. His heart was beating very fast, and a cold sweat ran down his back. The forest had become completely black, but Agouhanna knew his way very well now, and finally he no longer heard the heavy step which had chilled him with fear. He decided to rest for a bit, but suddenly he tripped over a heavy root and fell onto a dead tree. As he fell, he skinned his thigh against a dry branch.

He got up and started off at a walking pace, in order to catch his breath. While walking he felt a gentle warmth trickling down his thigh. He slid his hand along his thigh—it felt soaking wet. He looked at it; it was full of blood. The sight of his own blood sent shivers down his spine. But he kept on walking anyway—the vil-

lage was no longer very far off and his lynx eyes
enabled him to make out where he was at, just
as if it were broad daylight. He felt very hot,
then very cold. A fierce fever was consuming
him. His thigh was swelling up. He had to cross
a stream; the water froze his limbs. When he
gained the riverbank, he could no longer con-
tinue to walk. He began to crawl. Suddenly a
pain stabbed him in the loins. His face slipped
down into the mud. Agouhanna moved no
more.

When he awoke, the young Iroquois saw the
high ceiling of his parents' cabin, channeled
with heavy branches. Turning his head with an
effort, he saw his mother seated on the ground
at his side. Farther off, he could make out his
father, seated by the fire, his legs folded beneath
him. He was smoking his pipe and seemed lost
in a dream.

Agouhanna had no idea how he had come to
be there, in his parents' home. It seemed to him
that he must be dreaming. When he had fallen
asleep in the forest with his face in the mud, he
had not reckoned on the fact that he was less
than a hundred feet from the edge of the wood
which gave on the fort. The next morning, a
group of hunters had found him asleep and carried him home. For two whole days, he had
been deep in a feverish sleep. His mother

remained continuously at his bedside, watching his face for signs of life.

As soon as his mother saw that he had opened his eyes, she gave a start of joy, leaned over him, and, with her cool gentle hand, touched his forehead. It gave the boy a great feeling of well-being and a keen pleasure. He smiled at his mother. Then his hands slid back and forth over something very soft, and he recognized his fine bearskin. Yes, he was really home—it was not a dream.

He moved his lips, but could not speak—his mouth was too dry, and his lips hurt him terribly. He made a gesture, and his mother understood that he wanted some water. She ran to look for a wooden bowl, dipped it into a barken bucket filled with water, raised up her child, and held the bowl to his parched lips.

Agouhanna's mother was so happy to see her child return to life that tears spurted from her black shallow eyes and coursed down over her dark prominent cheekbones. At the same time she murmured, "He's alive, he's alive!"

His father did not move. Nothing changed in his face. He continued to smoke his pipe calmly, as if nothing were happening. However, he was deeply disturbed. When the hunters had found his son, unconscious at the edge of the forest, near the village wall, it was only the second day of the ordeal that was supposed to last for three days. Why had he come back so soon, the old chieftain asked himself, even if they *had* found his boy with bloody hands and swollen feet. What had happened? Had he been attacked? Had he been afraid?

These questions were on the tip of the commander's tongue, but he would never have deigned to utter them. A warrior did not ask such questions. For the moment, what mattered was that his son was alive. Even though he was troubled, this did give him a deep and silent joy, which—behind his impassive expression—he desired to cling to for himself alone.

Little by little, Agouhanna regained his strength. Then, one day, he ventured outdoors. He was still weak, and felt dazed by the brilliant daylight. It was a lovely sunny day, and the summer air smelled good. He walked into the tall grass with uncertain steps, so happy that he felt in his heart a desire to leap high into the air, like a bird. Around him was everything which could enchant the heart of a little Iroquois after having been shut up for weeks in an uncomfortable cabin—birds, flowers, fragrant herbs, trees, sun, and insects.

All of a sudden, Agouhanna stopped, frozen in his tracks. His heart began to pound in his chest. A group of boys was advancing toward him. At their head he recognized Owl, son of the witch doctor. Agouhanna didn't like this group, especially the witch doctor's son, whom he found insolent and nastily jeering. When he was with them he always felt ill at ease and inferior. His first reaction was to look for a place to hide, but it was too late—the gang had spotted him.

They surrounded him.

"What kind of huge beast did you meet in the forest?" the witch doctor's son asked him with a mocking air.

"A bear or a squirrel?" another one threw at him.

"If you killed an animal, how come you didn't bring it with you?" Owl went on, "I suppose it was too big."

All the boys began to laugh at the top of their lungs. Agouhanna kept his mouth tightly shut. He knew that Owl had a grudge against him for many reasons, particularly because he was the chief's son and especially because he had carried off the prize after the first ordeal. He was envious of Agouhanna. He was making use of his influence on the gang to poke fun at the son of the commander.

Besides, Agouhanna was afraid to provoke him, all the more because they were all outside the stockade and rather far from the village. If they did attack him, there would be nobody to defend him.

"Answer right now," Owl ordered, "otherwise we'll tie you to this tree and leave you to spend the night alone in the forest."

At these words Owl and his young companions quickly seized Agouhanna and stuck his shoulders against a tree. Owl uncoiled a long rawhide lash which he had been wearing around his waist. He used it to tie Agouhanna's hands and feet and then wound it around the tree.

Little Doe came along unexpectedly. She cried out insults at them and ordered them to free Agouhanna. The gang began to laugh.

"What about it—can't you defend yourself alone?" They flung out at their prisoner. "Do you have to have help from girls?"

Then they seized hold of Little Doe, who struggled tooth and nail against them, and tied her to the same tree as Agouhanna.

"There you go—you're bound together. Now you're married, thanks to us," Owl jeered.

Laughing, they danced wildly around the tree in a circle and broke into a wedding song that they had often heard at the time of marriage festivals.

Suddenly White Eagle and a group of his friends arrived on the run, drawn by the laughter, shouting, and singing. The two groups faced each other and began to jostle one another. White Eagle struck out on all sides, then jumped on Owl and dragged him to the ground. Owl, feeling that he had the worst of it, asked for mercy. White Eagle let him go, crying out, "Go on, beat it! And watch out—next time I won't let you go so easily."

Owl, followed by his gang, went off, woefully and sadly humiliated. An Indian cannot beg for mercy—it is a serious offense against his honor. So Owl had to maintain a tenacious and pitiless grudge with regard to White Eagle—especially since he had been humiliated in front of a girl, and a girl who believed that she was brave into the bargain!

White Eagle's companions didn't dare laugh when Owl sneaked off with his gang. They were glued to the spot by White Eagle's audacity—to hit the son of a chieftain was bad enough; but the son of a witch doctor! Anything could happen, a catastrophe could befall the village, if the witch doctor turned his hand to calling forth the evil spirits. Every Indian believed that unquestioningly. And they trembled at nothing so much as the thought of the hideous mask that he put on at the time of the ceremonies.

A heavy silence fell on the children. Suddenly White Eagle started to laugh—had they forgotten the prisoners? They all happily set about freeing Agouhanna and Little Doe.

She went off with the friends of White Eagle without even thanking him for having rescued her—White Eagle's intervention had humiliated her as well. She didn't want anyone to defend her. Remaining behind with Agouhanna, White Eagle stretched out on the ground, face down, and without a word began to chew on a blade of grass. Standing before him, Agouhanna said simply, "White Eagle, you've helped me again. I owe you a great deal."

Not bothering to raise his head, continuing to chew nonchalantly on the blade of grass, White Eagle seemed indifferent to these words. His thoughts appeared to be elsewhere. After some long moments of silence, he spat out the grass and said slowly, without moving, his eyes fixed on the dark mass of the forest, "Then try to become a man."

"You can be a man without being a hunter or a warrior."

Surprised, White Eagle said, "I don't understand what you're saying."

"Neither do I. And I don't know why I said

it. But it does seem to me that it should be possible."

"You say a lot of things that I've never heard before, and you seem to know more than the rest of us, Agouhanna. Just the same, you ought to try to be brave. It ought to be easy for you— you're the son of a great commander."

"That's just it—I don't feel like the son of a great commander."

Shocked, White Eagle could not refrain from asking, "Do you really admit something like that?"

"I don't like violence, or hunting, or warfare. What's more, I can't control my fear—it's within me, and it's stronger than I."

White Eagle tore up a handful of grass, threw it to the wind, then said in a calm voice, "If you don't become a brave, you'll be worth less in my eyes than the rootless grass that the wind carries away."

Then White Eagle went off, without even turning around once to acknowledge the repeated calls of his friend.

Remaining alone, Agouhanna allowed himself to fall to the ground, his face buried in his folded arms. He wept. He found life too complicated. Why wasn't he like the others? He could make nothing of it.

"What, are you crying? A future warrior, crying?"

Surprised, Agouhanna turned over on his back. Through his tears and the tall grass, he perceived the cool and determined face of Little Doe, who stood erect before him. Without answering the little girl's question, he pushed himself up with his elbows, then pivoted and sat down on a tree trunk. In one quick motion Little Doe sat down beside him.

"Why are you crying?" she insisted.

"I don't know. Maybe because I feel that I'm different from other people."

"You don't like hunting. I know that."

"I *don't* like hunting."

"You hate fighting."

"Yes, I hate fighting."

"How complicated it all is! Here I am, a girl, and I love to hunt and fight. How I would have loved it, just before, to jump on Owl and give him a good thrashing! When I saw that you were their prisoner, I was just enraged. I wanted to fight them all."

That really made Agouhanna laugh—and Little Doe had to also.

"Little Doe, you're really an evil spirit," Agouhanna concluded, between bursts of laughter, "a terror of the forest."

"Yes, I *am* an evil spirit, and a terror, and lots more than that. And if I had been a boy instead of a girl, I'm sure that I would have become the greatest commander of our tribe . . . Oh! Forgive me, Agouhanna—I was forgetting your father."

Thinking that she had gone too far, Little Doe lowered her eyes, which were like glowing coals, and was apparently very abashed. In order to reassure her, Agouhanna said to her, "If my father heard you, he'd smile—and remember, ordinarily he never smiles. He wouldn't punish you, because he's just, and he admires boldness. You're a really brave Little Doe."

At these words, the little girl flushed angrily. She shot back scornfully, with lightning in her eyes, "Little Doe, Little Doe! What a name! Why did they give me such a ridiculous name? It would have been all right for a potscourer or a corn-husker, but for me? Really!"

Agouhanna was really amused by the little girl's raging expression. Taking her gently by the hand, he said to her in a tone that was half jesting, half serious, "If I ever do succeed my father as chief of the village, I'll marry you, I'll name you commander of my warriors, and I'll give you another name."

Both intrigued and incredulous, Little Doe

blurted out, "Would you, Agouhanna, the great commander's son, really do all that?"

"Wait, I'll prove it to you."

As he said this, Agouhanna spat on a dry branch and threw it away. This gesture reassured Little Doe somewhat.

"And what will you name me?" she asked again.

"There are many moons for me to think of that. Listen, I promise you to think about it for one whole day between two moons."

This idea made them both laugh. After a moment, Little Doe grew serious again and asked, "But what about you—when we're married, what will you do? You'll take your father's place as chieftain of the village and commander of our warriors—"

"No, never, not that!" the young Iroquois cried vehemently. "I won't become a warrior for anything in the world. Why should it be necessary, ever since the beginning of our tribe, for all of our boys to become hunters and warriors just because they're boys? Couldn't we devise some other skill for them, one fine day?"

"I don't understand your attitude, but doubtless you're right. It's the same thing for girls like me. Why are we all destined for the most degrading work just because we're females? It's all ridiculous and stupid."

45

They heard some voices calling out to them—no doubt people knew that they were together. Little Doe sighed heavily, squeezed Agouhanna's shoulders with a sudden gesture, gave him an impetuous kiss on the cheek, and ran off toward the village.

Agouhanna remained there for a long time, lying in the grass, still feeling Little Doe's cool firm lips on his cheek, and daydreaming of the beautiful and high-spirited warrior that she could become. He fell asleep with a smile on his lips.

Then came the time of the next-to-the-last ordeal. The young Iroquois who emerged victorious from this trial would receive the title of warrior, with all the privileges that were accorded to the defenders of the tribe. Warriors never worked, for example, and had slaves to serve them. For the most part, the slaves were former prisoners of war.

This is what the next-to-the-last ordeal consisted of: In the course of a ceremony planned for the purpose, the young participants had to hold a burning coal in their hands for as long as they possibly could. The one who held the coal between his hands for the longest period was customarily considered as a future commander. They made the ordeal the occasion for a great nocturnal festival.

Those who were successful in the trial received from the grand commander the title of warrior and a crown of glittering feathers, then were grouped together in the center of the gathering to perform the dance of the warriors around a roaring blaze. Then the entire assemblage surrounded them, encouraged them with shouts and applause, and pelted them with flowers.

When the great day of the ordeal arrived, there was a regular coming and going in the village. Everyone brought something. All day long, they were carting dry wood and making a vast pyre from it in the middle of the village square.

A little before sundown, the boys who were going to undergo the ordeal had to put on their finest attire. Each family competed in variety of decorations and choice of colors. The September evening promised to be gentle, luminous, and warm. The public square, alive with numerous shadows, was lazily lit with great smoking torches. Everything was silent.

Suddenly there was a great cry in the night.

The old chieftain had just seized one of the smoking torches planted in the ground. It was the signal for the festival. He hurled the torch into the pyre. After considerable sparkling and smoking, a long flame slid like a serpent between the dry branches; then, breaking free, leaped toward the dark sky pierced with stars. At the sight of the high flame, clear and hot, the cries of the crowd redoubled as a sign of their delight. Soon the pyre was nothing more than an immense furnace violently illuminating the entire square.

Then the old commander seated himself on an enormous, almost square stone, before the pyre. The elders of the village squatted on the ground on either side of him. Warriors who had already taken part in combat stood aligned behind the commander and the elders. Everyone else made a circle around the pyre. The young Iroquois who had to undergo the ordeal stayed together in a corner, forming a closed, silent, and fearful group—each of them was asking himself with anxiety how he would emerge from this terrible trial.

At a sudden sign from the commander, a warrior broke free from the group and, in the midst of a profound silence, advanced toward the boys. Instinctively the boys recoiled a bit, each one afraid of being chosen as the first. The war-

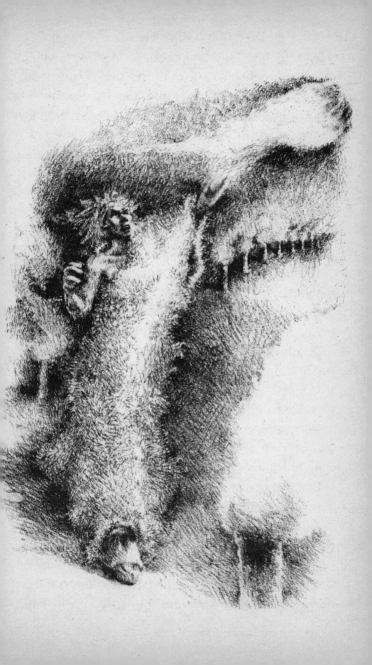

rior picked one at random, took him by the hand, and led him before the commander. Another warrior dug into the furnace with a long pole flattened at the end like an oar, and drew forth a glowing coal. When he presented the flat end of the pole to the child, black smoke was escaping from the wood singed by the coal. The child jumped back, terrified by the sight.

Without a word, the warrior led him back to his group, leaving him to try again, since his task was more difficult that that of the others, who wound up by becoming accustomed to the spectacle.

A second one presented himself to the commander. This time the child extended his hands, palms up. The commander himself took the smoking pole that the warrior offered him, held it motionless above the boy's hands, then slowly rocked the end up and down: the hot coal fell into the lad's hands. The knack was in keeping it as long as possible, without letting it fall to the ground, by passing it very quickly from one hand to the other; for in addition it was essential that the child's face should betray no sign of pain.

When the coal touched the child's hands, he remained impassive. But after two passes he let the coal fall. However, he had held on to it long enough without showing the least sign of pain, and they had him sit near the commander, thereby showing that he had succeeded in the trial and that henceforth he would be considered as a warrior. The crowd applauded and shouted with joy.

The three boys who followed failed their test; then two others succeeded. Little Doe stood in the first row of spectators. She cried out and applauded furiously for those who succeeded in the ordeal. Suddenly she stood stock-still, and her face grew serious. She had just seen Agouhanna advance toward his father. All eyes were riveted on the boy. He proceeded gravely, with considerable grace and dignity, in the midst of a profound silence. Then he halted, impassive, before his father.

But when he saw the smoking oar swinging toward him, Agouhanna was overcome with panic. At the thought of touching this red-hot, burning coal, he lost consciousness. He fell forward at his father's feet, face down in the dust.

There was a moment of confusion and great excitement among everyone present. Everyone —including the old chieftain and the witch doctor—thought that an evil spirit, not wanting him to be touched by the fire, had seized the child and flung him down to the ground. Since they feared the evil spirits, no one wanted to approach the child while he remained unconscious. Even the old commander kept his distance.

Only Little Doe had moved forward, fearlessly. She knelt next to Agouhanna and raised his head, resting it on her arm. She was doing what not even Agouhanna's father would have dared to do. The old commander looked on without saying a word, but indulgently, as though he admired and approved the little girl's courage.

When Agouhanna opened his eyes, the first thing that he saw was the anxious, pretty face of Little Doe bent over him, and it reassured him. On discovering that he was regaining consciousness, the little girl uttered a cry of joy.

At that instant, the commander gave a signal to the warriors. In the midst of a general silence, they approached Agouhanna with great respect, set him on his feet, washed his face, and bade him sit beside the chief. The significance of this was that from now on Agouhanna was to be considered as a warrior and as the successor to the great commander, even though he had not undergone the ordeal. He had been chosen by the spirits and thus was unlike the others—that sufficed. Therefore it was necessary to respect him as the future chief.

The ceremony began again as if nothing had happened. It was the turn of Owl, the witch doctor's son. Owl came forward full of assurance. He took his place, stiffly erect, before the old commander. When the smoking oar arose before him, Owl thrust out his arms firmly. The hot coal fell into his hands, cupped to form a bowl. At once he attempted to make the ember jump from one hand to the other, but his hands were too sensitive. Unable any longer to bear this violent pain, he had to let the coal fall after only a few passes. He had half failed, half passed the ordeal, but was allowed to enter the row of warriors just the same, no doubt because of the fact that he was the son of the witch doctor, whom everyone feared intensely. Nevertheless Owl was himiliated and infuriated, for he had wanted to keep the coal in his hands for so long that it would have been impossible to do other than recognize him as the future commander.

Then came White Eagle's turn. He had often practiced this game in secret with Little Doe. He made the red-hot coal leap for so long between his hands, which were beating the air in machinelike fashion, that he won the frenzied applause of the crowd. Even the old commander had difficulty in concealing an expression of admiration, which wrinkled his face—customarily as motionless as still water—with a shiver of joy.

White Eagle quickly passed on into the ranks

of the warriors, and was given as much respect as a future commander. Owl gave White Eagle a ferocious look. He detested him and wished him dead for having succeeded at what he himself had desired so dearly. He had much less of a grudge against Agouhanna, whom he regarded as a milksop.

During this time, three of the last contestants were passing into the row of warriors.

A surprise awaited the audience.

When the last one had entered the ranks of the warriors at a sign from the old chieftain, Little Doe suddenly leaped up and planted herself before the commander. Very proudly and stiffly, she held out her hands in a voluntary and audacious gesture. The entire assemblage began to laugh noisily—all except the old commander. He extended his right hand and laid it gently on the little girl's beautiful, shining black hair; then he shook his head. The little girl knelt before the old man, begging him to allow her to undergo the ordeal.

Since Indians are accustomed to refuse nothing to their children, the commander signaled to the warriors to approach with a glowing coal. He believed that at the approach of the smoking pole, Little Doe would take fright and flee. Instead, quick as a flash, the little girl seized the glowing coal and made it leap between her hands so swiftly, and for so long, and with such skill, smiling all the while at the chief and his son, that a murmur of admiration arose from the crowd. When she allowed the coal to fall, she saw tears in the eyes of the old commander, and she was very proud.

Carried away by a feat unique in the history of the tribe, the warriors lifted the little girl high in their arms and passed her along to the end of the row.

This striking event created a grave problem. Never had a woman been a warrior in the tribe. A woman was supposed to do domestic chores and manual labor—but to make war, never!

The chief asked in a fatherly way, "Why have you done this?"

"Because I want to be a warrior," answered Little Doe unhesitatingly.

There it was. That was precisely the problem, and the old commander had guessed it exactly. Faced with Little Doe's categorical declaration, the commander decided to bring together on the spot his grand council of the elders and deliberated with them in complete secrecy, while the crowd discussed the case of the little girl. The elders, who ordinarily seldom said more than a word or two during these deliberations, became very verbose.

After lengthy discussions, the council of the

elders decided in its wisdom that Little Doe, because of the exceptional qualities of bravery that she had displayed, would henceforth be one of the warrior caste, despite her being female. Thus from now on she would have the right to wear the gala adornments, the headdress, and the warriors' weapons at the official tribal festival. She would participate in the warriors' tournaments as well as in the defense of the village, but she would never take part in the aggressive campaigns against the tribe's enemies. In addition, it was decreed that, like every woman of the tribe, when she married she would have to see to the household duties.

When the old commander gave the signal to the little girl to take her place among the warriors, a disapproving murmur arose from the assemblage. They had never seen such a thing! In the festivals and the tournaments, the village would be ashamed to see one of its young girls dressed as a warrior. What would the people of other villages say? Everyone had his own remarks to make.

But the old commander and the elders had made their decision. So Little Doe came forward gravely to range herself alongside the warriors, despite the murmurs of the crowd. As if by chance, she found herself next to Agouhanna, who was overflowing with admiration for the pluck and courage of the little girl. He gave her a sidelong glance in silence, a glance so filled with respect and love that their hands met and clasped.

Agouhanna and Little Doe would never forget this evening. They were two hearts beating strongly in the midst of the stars, the multicolored feathers, the flames, and the muscular warriors who had donned their masks and fierce weapons; two children who loved each other and had come together to promise themselves to each other forever.

In consequence, Little Doe could be seen taking part in all of the young braves' hunting expeditions. She really made life a burden for her mother, who spent her time calling after her and looking all over for her, even in the wood, to get her to do the smallest household chore. Yet everyone grew accustomed to the idea, and it amused everyone—except her poor mother. But she wound up by gladly forgiving her daughter, especially when the little girl brought back more game than any of her companions and succeeded, all by herself, in supplying all of her household's food needs.

Agouhanna accompanied Little Doe on almost all of these hunting trips, but he never brought back any game. Yet his parents did not reproach him for this. He was satisfied to aim at trees with his bow. Often he lay down in the tall grass or on a moss-covered boulder, daydreaming or observing the flight of the birds, the exhausting labor of an ant, or the patience and skill of a spider, while Little Doe was hunting. He could not bring himself to kill an animal. But he never reproached Little Doe for this. When she emerged from a thicket, waving the product of her hunt at arm's length, Agouhanna contented himself with looking at her and smiling, full of admiration for such liveliness, joy, and health. Then he arose, stretching, slowly and lazily, and the two children returned to the village by countless little byways, since they had all the time in the world.

During the summer and fall, all the inhabitants of the village who were fit labored to accumulate stores of corn, venison, and fish for winter. All, that is, except for Agouhanna. Not only didn't he want to kill the beasts of the forest or to catch the fish of streams and lakes, but in addition he had deeply rooted prejudices against work. Work was repugnant to him. Besides, he was clumsy at everything. The only skills he felt he had were for thinking and dreaming.

His sensitivities had been sharpened and his imagination developed by the tales of the war-like exploits of his father and the elders (even if he himself had never experienced them), by the legends of the tribal gods, the mysterious world of the dead and the spirits, the rich and wild nature which surrounded them, and even his uncontrollable fear of everything and nothing. He spent his time making up tales in which the weak wound up with the upper hand, and setting them to music.

Everyone, including his father the old commander, forgave him for his attitude, for he enchanted them during the long winter evenings when they gathered together in the cabin to keep warm, to eat, and to hear stories and songs. The charm of Agouhanna's tales and songs, and the body heat emitted by everyone, warmed the assemblage even more than the fire of the main hearth which smoked up the cabin, and around which the old people drowsed.

No one knew any longer whether Agouhanna was cowardly or brave, but they had finally accepted him for what he was. If he didn't bring back game to nourish their bodies, he provided ample food to refresh and sustain their spirits. As for the business of the hot coals, it had only reinforced the aura of mystery and respect that already surrounded the young poet—for that is really what Agouhanna had become—a poet.

Around the age of thirteen, Agouhanna and his companions had to undergo the final ordeal that every young Iroquois was obliged to undergo in order to complete his education. This is what the last ordeal consisted of: The adolescent would go off into the forest alone. There he would construct a little tent in which he had to remain, bedded down, for eight to ten days without taking any nourishment at all. During all this time, he could only pray and try to dream of a spirit which would be his lifelong guardian. After many days' fasting, a young boy, weakened and feverish, would begin to have hallucinations. Whatever object—whether an animal, a plant, or anything else—haunted him most frequently during his dreams would become his guardian angel for life.

Among the Indians, belief in these guardian angels was so strong that they habitually attributed any remarkable achievement by a tribe member to his guardian. Often it even happened that a young Indian would change his name to that of his guardian.

Every boy would prepare himself for this adventure with considerable seriousness and a certain anxiety, because it was one of the main events of their youth, and for many of them was going to influence the rest of their life. Their fate would depend in large part on the guardian who was going to befall them. Even Agouhanna was excited by it. But the trouble was that he had never lost any of his sickly fear. He loved the forest more and more—but with company.

So Agouhanna was tormented in spirit. On the one hand, he was dying to know who his guardian would be; and on the other, he was chilled with terror at the thought of that long solitude in the forest. It was out of the question to stay in the village, since he would then have to spend the rest of his life without a guardian—aside from the fact that this time his cowardliness would surely be unmasked. Owl would not miss the opportunity to make him the laughingstock of the entire village.

Agouhanna could see only one way to resolve his problem—he'd have to have recourse one last time to the friendship of White Eagle. It would be a painful step for Agouhanna to take. He'd be ashamed, to be sure, but so much the worse for him!

White Eagle refused point-blank to share Agouhanna's tent, or to have Agouhanna share his. However, after many discussions in which the friendship that had always bound them together underwent some strain, the two boys arrived at a compromise. Each one would build his own tent, but each would be located within earshot of the other.

On the specified day, all the boys who were going to participate in the final ordeal were brought together in the center of the village, dressed in all their finery, with bows, arrows, and tomahawks. They also wore rolled-up deer-skins which would be serving as their tents. All the people of the village had gathered about them to give them their blessings and to bid them farewell. At a sign from the old chieftain, the group got under way, crossed the village, passed through the great gate to the cheers of the crowd, then dispersed in the dense forest.

Agouhanna and White Eagle were quickly reunited, in accordance with their understanding. They walked swiftly, one in front of the other. The heat of the July sun, tempered by the coolness of the undergrowth, joyously invigorated their healthy young bodies. Happy, they flexed their growing muscles like young animals, overflowing with liveliness and plunging into the woods as if they were discovering a paradise.

They called out loudly in order to hear the echoes respond to them.

The two friends chose a wooded hillside overlooking a lake to establish their quarters. Each helping the other to set up their tents, they began by cutting sturdy branches which would serve as supports for their deerskins. They were careful to implant these supporting branches firmly in the ground, and to sew the skins to the branches so that everything should hold fast. Each one made a comfortable bed of moss. A hide served as a door. The hide could be attached from the inside in such a fashion as to prevent animals from getting into the tent during the night.

When everything was finished, each withdrew to his tent, after gripping the other's shoulder as a sign of brotherhood.

Once inside his little tent, Agouhanna firmly attached the hide, which closed off the entrance, and stretched out on his bed of moss. Even though his friend was not far off, Agouhanna, lying on his back, felt his heart beating very rapidly. He was overcome by a kind of anxiety, like that which would sometimes overtake him at twilight.

After some hours, it grew completely dark. The little opening he had left at the top of the tent was not enough to get rid of the heat which

prevailed. The youth was soaking with sweat.
He could hear all kinds of strange noises around
him, and they terrified him.

Several times he came near calling out to his
friend; but he held back, more afraid of ridicule
than of the unknown around him. It was already
humiliating enough that he had had to ask his
friend to stay nearby. His ears on the alert for
every suspicious sound, his large doe's eyes star-
ing into the night, he held his tongue and shud-
dered. He wound up by falling asleep.

When he awoke, a pole light was whitening
the stretched deerskins, the birds were singing,
and a gentle freshness reigned in the tent. Morning had arrived at last! Agouhanna stretched his
limbs and breathed easily. His sleep had calmed
him and the new-born day was giving him courage.

Toward midday, the heat in the tent became
unbearable. Agouhanna could scarcely breathe,
the air was so heavy. His body was streaming
with sweat even though he did not move about.
To pass the time he began to compose a song.
He felt with all his soul that his spirit was escaping through the little blue opening of the roof
which gave on the sky and lost itself in the infinite.

With the coming of evening he fell asleep
effortlessly. But in the middle of the night he

was suddenly awakened by steps around the tent so heavy that they made the dry branches snap. A long, raucous sigh accompanied these noisy footsteps. Suddenly the movement stopped. Agouhanna, terrified, had the feeling that a big snout was rubbing against the taut hide of the tent.

The beast's breathing made the deerskin vibrate, and Agouhanna's sensitive nose seemed to sniff the odor of bear. For there was no longer any possible doubt—it really was a bear. Agouhanna even heard some rumbling growls. The young Iroquois thought that he would die of fear even before falling under the animal's claws. But the beast wandered off with no more ado, just as it had come.

Agouhanna stayed awake for a long time, his ears sharpened and his body tensed with fear. Finally he fell asleep.

The following night, the same thing happened —and then the animal wandered off again, as it had the previous night. And so it was on the third, fourth, and fifth nights. But the more often the event occurred, the less afraid Agouhanna became, and the more quickly he could go to sleep again.

When he awoke on the morning of the sixth day, Agouhanna felt dizzy and feeble. His mouth was pasty and dry. His body felt at once riveted to its bed of moss and floating in the air in the middle of the tent; at once heavy and rigid as maple wood, and light as a spiraling coil of smoke. He had consumed nothing at all for five days. During all this time, he had only moistened his lips with some brackish water from a leather bucket at his bedside. The long fast was beginning to have its effect.

Agouhanna's mind had become so alert and so sharp that the youth could call up an animal and, closing his eyes, see it in perfect clarity before him, in every detail. It was in this way that the idea of a bear came back to him strongly, and returned more and more often to his mind. Soon it was no longer possible for him to think of anything else.

For Agouhanna did not doubt it any longer —it was surely a bear that returned every night to prowl around his tent. A thousand details returned to his mind, and proved it to him clearly. In a flash it became clear to him, with the utmost sharpness, that the only object which had been haunting him ever since his first night in the tent was a bear. If he could dream of this animal, the bear would become his guardian for life.

All day long he thought of nothing but the

bear. But strangely enough, the bear did not come the following night. Agouhanna slept without dreaming.

On the eighth day, feverish, discouraged, weak, soaked with a cold sweat, almost paralyzed, his body shaken by fits of shivering, the young Iroquois concentrated his efforts for the entire day on calling up the bear, begging the Great Manitou to make it his guardian.

Then night fell again. Agouhanna both desired and feared the visit of the bear. Extremely agitated on his resting place, Agouhanna could not get to sleep. Finally, though, the bear did not come, and Agouhanna wound up by falling asleep.

In his sleep, he dreamed that he was squatting in the grass before his tent. It was a mild and radiant day. The sunlight seemed to make every object look priceless. Agouhanna had the feeling that he was floating above the ground, as if his body had become a spirit. He was happy, and perfectly calm.

Suddenly, twenty paces from him, he saw the foliage of a thick bush slowly part. An enormous, dark mass emerged—it was an immense bear. On catching sight of the young Iroquois, the bear neither slowed nor hastened its pace. The bear headed straight for him. Strange to say, Agouhanna felt no fear at all. On the con-

trary, he looked on its arrival as the most natural thing in the world, as if he had been expecting—and even welcoming—this visit.

The bear stopped a few feet from the boy. Then it sat down slowly and began to growl, while shaking its head from one side to the other. The growls were confusing at first; then distinct words were mingled with them. Finally the growls gave way to words spoken in a gruff, deep voice; and Agouhanna had no trouble understanding their meaning. The bear was speaking the language of his tribe, which did not surprise Agouhanna in the least.

The bear began to give the young Iroquois advice with the greatest friendliness, suggesting to him authoritatively that he ought never again to fear anything at all in life, and that, if he were always to behave in that way, he would be respected by everyone and would become a great personage among his people.

"You are Agouhanna," he said, "which is to say a brave among braves, as your name signifies. Never forget it!" Then the bear added, slowly scratching his right armpit with his long glittering claws, "If ever you become afraid, call on me. You will not see me, but you will hear my growling wherever you may be, and when you hear it you will no longer feel fear. From this moment on, I shall be your guardian, and I shall remain your guardian until the end of your life."

After these words, and after scratching himself very deliberately once again, the massive bear fell back heavily on his forepaws, made a half turn, and disappeared from sight with the ponderous and clumsy gait with which he had appeared.

When Agouhanna awoke, the sun was already high in the sky. A bird was singing throatily, as if it wanted to awaken the entire world. Agouhanna stretched slowly, then followed with his eyes the complicated filigree work of the stretched and all but transparent deerskin that the sun's rays were illuminating. He felt somewhat bewildered.

Suddenly, his entire dream came back to him. There was no longer any possible doubt—he now had his guardian, and it was a very huge and very powerful bear. He recalled clearly what the bear had said to him in his dream: "Call on me whenever you're afraid—and when you hear my growls, you'll no longer be afraid. I shall be your guardian for the rest of your life."

Agouhanna smiled. He felt happy and calm. From now on, he would never be afraid of anything.

When he wanted to get up, so that he could go out and shout his joyous news to White

Eagle, he could not move. His head, and his entire body, were so heavy and so sore that he could not make the slightest movement. His lips were dry, his eyes burning with fever. Then he remembered that he had not taken any nourishment for eight days.

Agouhanna remained motionless for hours. Then, after many painful efforts, he succeeded in turning over on his stomach. Finally he was able to raise himself up and sit down on his sleeping mat. At the same time, he had to stretch out once again, for he simply felt too dizzy.

But in spite of his aches and his exertions, he could not keep from smiling. Now he had become someone else, a being who would never again feel fear. Then he thought of his father, his mother, White Eagle, and Little Doe. How dear they were to his heart! How sweet, how comforting it would be to have their admiration as well as their love! Yes, he would be brave for them, but not brave in a violent way. He would be brave in a gentle way—in the love of his own people, and of nature.

Agouhanna was thinking of all this when he heard a clamor coming from far off, then drawing closer. Soon he could make out a warrior chant that he recognized—it had to be the warriors of the village, who were running through the forest to come to the aid of all those who had endured this last trial, in order to show them that the ordeal was over, to support their weakened bodies, and to bring them their first meal in more than a week.

All of a sudden, Agouhanna heard footsteps and voices around his tent; then a knife sliced through the lacing that held the tent closed, a muscular arm separated the deerskin, and the heads of two warriors, whom the young Iroquois recognized, appeared in the opening. Smiling, the warriors asked him if he could get up without help. Agouhanna gestured that he could not. Whereupon they raised up the tent and he found himself stretched out on his bed in the open air.

They helped him to sit up, then handed him some water. After that, they got him to swallow a sort of cold soup cooked with deer meat and corn. At first he had considerable difficulty in swallowing anything at all, for his lips and his throat were dry. Finally he was able to eat a bit, but more than anything he was thirsty.

The warriors made no comment on the presence of White Eagle, whose tent was not far from that of Agouhanna. They said only that he was not to move, and that they were going to leave him by himself while they took care of White Eagle.

The warriors accorded the same treatment to White Eagle. As a result, the two boys quickly regained their strength. The warriors wanted to take them right back to the village, but Agouhanna made it clear that he wanted to get together with White Eagle. The warriors strode off to the lake, which was a few hundred yards from where they were.

As soon as they were alone, the two friends soaked their heads, like young animals, in a clear spring near their tents. Then they began to laugh at the top of their lungs at the sight they made; their teeth gleamed in the sunlight. After that, they tumbled around on the cool moss that carpeted the banks of the stream. Each told the other of his days of solitude and fasting, and then of the revealing dream that he had had.

Woefully, White Eagle told how he had dreamed of a doe which came to drink from the spring near their tents. That was when he decided that he would keep his name and be his own guardian. He spoke of this in a calm voice, after having been teased by Agouhanna.

Then Agouhanna told about his own dream. He couldn't keep from repeating over and over, "You know, I'm not afraid any more now—and I'll never be afraid again."

White Eagle couldn't believe it.

So Agouhanna said to him forcefully, "It's

true, I assure you. I'm not afraid of anything any more. And to prove it to you, I'm going to stay here alone in the forest for a long time— maybe a month."

"A month!" cried White Eagle, incredulous.

"Yes, I'll probably stay here alone for a month, and after that I'll return to the village."

White Eagle was absolutely astonished at the change that had come over Agouhanna. Surprised and troubled, he asked, "But what are you going to do to feed yourself, to subsist on, alone here?"

"You know that I don't like to hunt or to kill animals. So I'll feed myself with plants, fruits, and roots. I want to meditate alone, and make up some stories and poems—that's what's more important to me than anything else in the world. Believe me, if I had to sacrifice the love I bear for Little Doe in order to do that, I'd do it without hesitation—and you know how much I love her."

"Yes, Agouhanna, you really were born to compose songs and stories, I've never doubted that for a single moment. That's the reason, above all, I swear it to you, why I was drawn to you in the first place. That's the reason I never really thought you were a coward. That's the reason, too, why I helped you when you asked me to."

With an affectionate gesture, Agouhanna put his arm around his friend's shoulders and held him fast. "I'm so indebted to you! I'll be grateful to you for my whole life!"

"Let's not speak of it any more, Agouhanna. All I want is your friendship. But that friendship makes me afraid for you—I'm afraid to leave you alone for such a long time in this out-of-the-way spot, far from our village. Supposing you're attacked by wild animals?"

"I'm not afraid of animals any more. Now, I'm their friend, they're mine—and they know it."

"And suppose some enemy warriors come by this way and see you? That would be the end for you—and what an awful end! Either they'd kill you, or they'd torture you, or they'd make you their slave," continued White Eagle, more and more upset.

"I don't want to think about those things. All I want is to be alone for a period of time."

"But what shall I tell your mother—and your father, our chieftain?"

"Repeat to them what I've just told you, and they'll understand. Talk to Little Doe too. She'll understand also. As far as the others are concerned, don't tell them anything."

"I'm still starving," White Eagle said. "What do you say we eat? I'm so hungry I could swallow three bears, ten hares, and two dozen partridges."

"As for me," Agouhanna began again, "I could eat that whole tree by the spring—leaves, roots, and all."

With a sweeping glance, both boys measured the giant elm that shaded the spring and then burst out laughing.

White Eagle suggested, "Let's eat some strawberries."

"What about the warriors who are waiting for us?" his friend remarked, looking at the two men seated near the lake.

"They'll wait for a while longer. Let's go, we'll make some cups for the strawberries."

"Yes, you're right," Agouhanna said, "There ought to be lots of strawberries around here."

Cutting some strips of birch bark, the two boys, weakened as they were, began enthusiastically to weave cups. The two warriors were content to observe them from a distance, shrugging their shoulders. They made a game of it, to see which one would finish first. White Eagle won the contest.

"You've always been more skillful than I," said Agouhanna, "but I'm not envious of you for it. That's the way it ought to be. There have to be people like you in a tribe, skillful at everything. If there were only clumsy people like me, what would happen to us?"

Growing serious once again, White Eagle replied, "There have to be people like you too. Otherwise our tribe just wouldn't be the same."

"Let's say that both of us are indispensable to each other—you to me, and me to you."

While chatting, the two friends had arrived at a clearing where the strawberries were strewn about the ground in lovely red patches. They fell happily to their knees and began to fill their containers with skill and speed, being very careful not to crush the berries. Quickly they filled their bark receptacles; then, seating themselves on the trunk of a dead tree, they sampled what they had picked.

After having eaten themselves sick on the berries, they rejoined the two warriors who had been patiently waiting for them. Not a word of reproach came from the two older men. Indeed, the adults were extremely patient with children, and it was rare that they upbraided them, no matter what the occasion.

Agouhanna told them of his decision to remain alone, at the edge of the lake. White Eagle would follow the warriors to the village. The warriors did not object to the decision, which they took for a whim. Among the Indi-

ans, one never thwarted a child's whim. Using
the hides of the two tents, the warriors built a
solid shelter to lodge and protect Agouhanna
against inclement weather and wild animals for
a long while. Once more, White Eagle expressed
his uneasiness. Agouhanna reassured him. He
even invited him to come visit him one day,
with Little Doe. White Eagle promised to do so.
Then they separated.

The two warriors often had to slow their
pace, since White Eagle still felt very weak and
had to rest repeatedly. They even had to hold
him up during long periods of their journey. His
legs trembled and sometimes seemed utterly
deprived of strength. But despite his suffering he
remained stoic, and uttered no complaint. The
sun went down, and soon night had arrived. But
fortunately the village was no longer far off.

All of a sudden they heard some hoarse, loud
cries—it was the rallying signal to call and guide
the laggards home. White Eagle felt great pleasure at this, but soon he was saddened again by
the thought that his best friend would be staying
on alone in the forest, far from the village that
was well protected, both by its high staked wall
and by its warriors. How Agouhanna had
changed! He had become so courageous that
White Eagle himself would never have dared to

undertake such a marathon—to spend part of the summer alone in the forest, with no protection, and so far from his people.

Suddenly White Eagle was anxious to see the villagers again, especially his parents and his friends. The encouraging cries were growing closer. Finally White Eagle could see, among the trees of the forest, the high dark wall of the village and the great open gate. All about, on the outside as well as on the inside, everything was humming with activity. Through the open gate, White Eagle could see a great fire in the middle of the square and the outlines of some adults and children dancing around it.

From the moment of his entrance, White Eagle was greeted as a hero. His parents squeezed him in their arms. Then he was surrounded and smothered with hugs by the people of the village. Most of the boys who had participated in the ordeal had already come back; forming a circle, they squatted near the fire, too weak to take part in the dance. White Eagle rejoined them. He was fearful of the moment when someone would ask him what he had dreamed of in the forest. It vexed him to have to say that he had dreamed of a doe—even if the doe symbolized gentleness and goodness, it could just as well stand for cowardice . . .

What difference did it make, anyway? After

all, didn't everyone in the village know that he was brave? His dream could also mean that he would become the protector of the weak.

By now it had grown completely dark. Only the huge bonfire lit up the faces and the dancing or squatting figures. Everybody except Agouhanna had come back to the village. Owl was trying hard to sneer at the absence of Agouhanna, asking whether he might have been eaten by a squirrel, or some other such wild animal. White Eagle still had not said a word about the absence of Agouhanna. Owl's mockery made his blood boil, but he controlled himself and remained silent. Now everyone was gathering around the young heroes who had returned from their long voyage to the land of dreams— for according to custom each one would recount his own dream around the great bonfire.

People were beginning to become seriously disquieted about Agouhanna's absence, even though the two warriors had announced that the youth wished to remain alone in the forest for some time. Agouhanna's parents seemed very anxious, but remained silent, asking no questions. It was customary for every youth who had undertaken the fast to begin talking only at the request of the chief.

But, confronted with the anxiety of Agouhanna's parents, White Eagle could remain silent no

longer. Suddenly he heard himself saying loudly, "I know why Agouhanna is not with us tonight."

"Why?" asked the chieftain in a neutral voice, not allowing any emotion to appear.

"Because his will has made that decision."

And White Eagle repeated what Agouhanna had ordered him to say. Except for the old chieftain and Agouhanna's mother, everyone exclaimed over the youth's will power, as well as his courage. Even Owl stood with his mouth agape.

Then they praised the young boy and congratulated the chieftain, who received these plaudits in silence, his face impassive. Was he pleased and happy with his son? Or annoyed? No one would ever know. Agouhanna's mother showed both her joy and her pride, but also her uneasiness at the thought of the dangers that lay in wait for her son, who was so young and frail, alone in the forest and without protection. But she did not dare to express her anxiety too sharply for fear of upsetting the old commander or making him depressed.

Little Doe was experiencing the same feelings of joy and anxiety. Agouhanna would have to overcome many dangers, but the one whom her heart had chosen had become courageous—that was what mattered above everything. She would go with White Eagle to see him in the forest.

Each boy took his turn before the chieftain to tell what had haunted him during his dreams. When White Eagle's turn came, his heart was beating very fast. He was ashamed to narrate his dream. The chief invited White Eagle to speak. The young boy hesitated. Standing before the chief, he lowered his head and said nothing.

Without losing patience, the chief once more urged him to speak, adopting a tone that was at once authoritative and fatherly. Finally White Eagle decided, and acknowledged what had haunted him in his dreams. Even while he was telling it, the boy was waiting fearfully for the awful moment when everyone would burst out laughing.

To his great astonishment, no one laughed. At the end of his story, White Eagle heard the chief's voice addressing him in a solemn tone. "My boy, it's a good sign that you should have dreamed of a doe. The doe will draw you toward gentleness, goodness, and love. With the strength, skill, and courage of the warrior, you will protect the weak—old people, women, children. My son, I predict to you that you will become a great military commander, at once feared like the lynx and loved like the doe."

White Eagle was overcome with astonishment. He remained where he was, abashed and happy. He would never have dared to hope for so much. The chief gave him a sign that he was free to leave, but then called him back.

During the entire ceremony, the chief had displayed neither impatience nor emotion with regard to his son. He had not asked a single question. His face impassive, he listened to the explanation of their dreams by those who followed. Then, after everyone had finished, he gestured to White Eagle to come still closer, and said to him, "You have seen Agouhanna."

"Yes. His tent wasn't far from mine." Seeing the chief knitting his brow, White Eagle hastened to add, "It was only by chance that we found ourselves not far from each other. It was only at the end of the fast, when we were leaving our tents, that we saw each other, with surprise. Then we fell into each other's arms."

"You're protesting too much, my boy," said the chief in a severe tone. "He told you that he would spend a good part of the time alone in the forest?"

"Yes."

"Fine. Now let us rejoin the others and take part in the festivities—you have earned it."

It was the custom to cook slowly an enormous stew of deer's meat and corn, seasoned with herbs, over the great fire in the middle of the square. After the ceremony the future warriors, famished from their long fast, squinted into the immense pot and helped themselves to gigantic portions. The villagers gathered around them to watch them eat, and were noisily delighted with the ferocious appetite of the young wolves, urging them on with a multitude of teasings. Consequently, certain of them became very ill as a result of all this gluttony, their stomachs not being accustomed to so much food.

White Eagle obeyed the chieftain and rejoined the group, but in spite of his fast he was not hungry. His thoughts were elsewhere—in the forest, with Agouhanna. Was he going to be able to take care of himself all alone? Supposing he were attacked by animals or got lost in the forest? White Eagle was asking himself all kinds of questions when, raising his eyes, he caught Little Doe's anxious look, which was fixed upon him. She was seated before him, a little way off, in the midst of a group of young girls.

Ordinarily, boys and girls did not mix during these ceremonies, but White Eagle could not resist. He arose, circled around the fire, and joined Little Doe. Taking advantage of the hubbub, she took him boldly by the hand and led him toward a nearby thicket. Once safe from prying eyes, she began to question him about Agouhanna.

"Do you know exactly where he is?"

"Yes, I know. His tent wasn't far from mine."

"Do you want to go see him?"

"Yes, we'll go."

"How brave Agouhanna has become! You know, I'm going to tell you a secret: I love Agouhanna very much. I'll never be able to love anyone else that much."

"I know that," White Eagle said with a smile.

"What do you mean, you know it?" Little Doe shot back angrily.

"You're the only one who doesn't see what everyone else sees."

Vexed, Little Doe compressed her lips. After she had taken so many precautions to hide her feelings!

Seeing the girl's disappointed expression, White Eagle began to laugh, then caressed her face, saying to her gently but seriously, "Little Doe, simply go on loving Agouhanna, and we all will love you still more."

"In that case, I'm going to tell you something

else about him. You know—even if he had never become brave, I would have loved him just the same."

"Anyway, from what I know of you, you really would have been able to be brave enough for the two of you."

Little Doe and White Eagle both started to laugh, then separated, each taking a different pathway back to the festivities.

As we know, Agouhanna's tent was near a lake. Seated on a stone at the water's edge, Agouhanna was doing some thinking. He asked himself if he had done the right thing in making this decision to remain alone for a good part of the summer. He had already spent ten days and, more important, ten nights alone in the forest. He ate well enough from fruits and herbs that grew wild, but the people of the village were now feasting all the time. At night, he was still afraid sometimes, but he called the bear, his guardian, and when it seemed to him that he could hear its growl, he would fall asleep again with no fear, reassured.

But he felt more and more shaken in his

resolve. He still had not had a visit from White Eagle or Little Doe. Maybe they hadn't been able to locate his tent. He thought often of his mother and of Little Doe. After having spent some time in fixing up his tent, gathering provisions of fruits and grasses, and exploring the area, he could no longer think of anything else to do. Very simply, he was getting bored. He had wanted to stay alone in the forest not only to prove to himself that he had become brave, but also to create some stories and songs. But, strangely enough, inspiration would not come to him.

He was growing very discouraged. He couldn't even dream of going right back to the village, for they would make fun of him. It would provide Owl with too perfect an opportunity to ridicule him. So he decided to stay on in the forest for another ten days, after which he would see.

Once he had made this decision, Agouhanna thought that it might be interesting to go off and explore the other side of the lake. Early that afternoon, he began to follow the lakeshore. Like every purebred Indian, Agouhanna took all kinds of precautions to avoid making the slightest sound while walking through the woods. Among Indians it was instinctive, surely a natural instinct of preservation.

After two hours of steady walking, Agouhanna found himself on the other side of the lake. Suddenly, he saw something move on one of the spits that projected out into the lake. From a distance, he could not clearly distinguish the shapes which were moving, but his instinct put him on guard. With infinite precaution, he moved toward the spit.

Suddenly, about five hundred feet ahead of him, he saw many tents raising their peaks heavenward. Around the tents, some men were going about their business noiselessly. They had to be enemies, for they had neither the clothing nor the appearance of the warriors of his own village.

Agouhanna's heart began to beat very rapidly. He was going to withdraw silently and return to the path he had followed, find his tent, and from there get back to the village without losing a minute in order to warn his people— even if it would be necessary to march all night through the forest. But suddenly powerful hands seized him by the shoulders. He wanted to cry out, but a hand was clapped over his mouth.

Then he was blindfolded and could see nothing more. Everything had happened with the speed of lightning and in absolute silence. Then he felt that they were carrying him off. After a long moment, he heard murmurs, and low voices uttering some words that he could not understand.

They made him sit down on the ground. Then, abruptly, they took off his blindfold. Agouhanna opened his eyes. At first he could see nothing, for his vision was obscured and his entire being was filled with confusion and bewilderment. Little by little, he began to distinguish some of the figures around him, then suddenly he could make out clearly some imposing warriors who were grouped about him. They were dark and heavily muscled. They were looking at him with curiosity, as if he were an animal or some rare object. Then they walked away from him, unconcerned, in order to get on with their various tasks.

Even though he believed that he had been brave, Agouhanna thought that he was going to die of fear. He didn't dare to cry or to make a gesture. What were they going to do with him? Kill him? Burn him alive? Stuff glowing coals into his mouth? All of the horror stories that had been told to him at night, around the fire, came back to him now. He felt himself growing weaker and weaker.

He closed his eyes tightly and called on the bear. He believed that he heard a kind of growling coming from far off, and it comforted him. He felt less alone, and more calm. After some real effort, he succeeded in opening his eyes. He began to observe what was going on around him.

No one was paying any attention to him. Some were putting up a tent that was smaller than the rest. Others were preparing a fire, taking considerable trouble to camouflage it. Still others were driving into the ground a great wooden pole, carved all over with colored masks, one more fearsome-looking than the next. And yet others were coming back from the lake with some fish that they had just caught.

After long hours seated on the ground, observing what was going on around him, Agouhanna saw the sun go down behind the trees on the other side of the lake. Not for one instant did there pass through his mind the idea that he should have been able to try to escape. Nevertheless, he was not tied up, and they seemed to be ignoring him. But everything around him seemed so strange that the child asked himself if he were dreaming—or if all this was actually real. After all, his long days of fasting had given him so many hallucinations!

At the moment when Agouhanna was asking himself these questions, he saw all the warriors gathering together, before the pole covered with terrible masks. Then, stiff as statues, they began to chant a plaintive and very sweet song, punc-

tuated now and then by sharp accents, while the last rays of the setting sun struck the top of the pole. As soon as the sun had completely disappeared, the singing stopped.

One after the other, the warriors disappeared into one of the tents, the largest one, and reappeared with their bows, and their quivers filled with arrows. After that, forming a circle, each of them drew forth an arrow and, taking aim at the center of the circle, all shot at the same time, sinking their arrows into the ground. It gave the center of the circle the look of an enormous porcupine.

Agouhanna was so fascinated by these ceremonies, which were completely new to him, that he forgot to be afraid. He saw the warriors pull their arrows out of the ground, put them back into their quivers, then pile the quivers and the bows before the tent, which apparently served as their arsenal. Then he watched them heading toward the fire with some large green leaves in their hands. Making use of a branch, they pulled out some fish that were cooking under the ashes and, squatting on the ground, began to eat greedily. The fish had such an appetizing odor, and Agouhanna was so hungry!

Suddenly one of them arose, poked through the ashes, brought out a fish, came back to settle himself before the young Iroquois, and with a

gesture as graceful and courteous as if he were
begging the child to accept, offered Agouhanna
the fish, lying on a bed of green leaves.

The boy leaped at the fish, which was so hot
it all but escaped his grasp. Then he began to
devour it, chewing the fish voraciously. The
sight delighted the warriors, who began to laugh
raucously. Startled, Agouhanna stopped eating.
The laughter ceased, and the glances became
serious. The warriors made gestures with their
hands for the child to eat. Reassured, Agouhanna resumed eating, and wound up by
devouring the fish completely. Then they
brought him a bark goblet filled with water,
which he drank down at one gulp.

Stationing themselves at some distance from
the young boy, the warriors clustered together in
a circle and exchanged some words in low
voices. Suddenly two warriors left the group and
headed toward the child. To his surprise and his
great fear, they lifted him by the elbows and
carried him toward the little tent that the warriors had built before his very eyes. They put
him down inside it on a bed of pine boughs,
then secured the entrance very firmly, lacing
together the sides of the tent.

Once he was alone in the darkness of the tent,
Agouhanna was more afraid than ever. His
entire body was trembling on the bed of pine

boughs, and he was about to cry, when suddenly the bear came back to his mind. He called on it with all his heart, keeping his eyes tight shut. All of a sudden he heard a bear growling clearly, right near the tent. At this familiar growling, his heart beat very quickly, and he felt suffused with the greatest joy. He wasn't afraid any more!

Motionless on his bed, his arms folded behind his head, perfectly calm, the child began to think. Suddenly, for the first time, the thought crossed his mind that these warriors could only have one aim: to attack his village. At whatever cost, he was going to have to forewarn his people.

It was at this moment that young Agouhanna asked himself if he would be able to escape, and the sooner the better, since he no longer had more than one idea in mind—to get to his village before the enemy and save his people. If by some misfortune they got there before he did, they would surely massacre the entire village! They would take his people by surprise.

But even if he could escape from the tent and frustrate the vigilance of the enemy, would Agouhanna be able to find his way through the forest in utter darkness? Suddenly he remembered that this was the period of the full moon. Since the sky had been clear when they locked

him in the tent, he would certainly be able to see
as if it were broad daylight.

The only great difficulty, then, was to get out
of the tent and get away without attracting
attention. Even while he was considering all
these things, Agouhanna had distractedly
dropped his hand on a heavy branch which was
part of his makeshift bed. An idea came to him
—this branch could save him. With his hands
he felt the ground; it seemed rather soft. He
began to prune the branch, using his skill as a
child of the forest to avoid making the slightest
sound.

When he had gotten the branch whittled
down to a stick, the young Indian got down on
his knees and began to scrape the ground, near
the tent wall. He put in long and very patient
hours at this silent labor—the least noise could
have betrayed him. He had dug a hole which
was big enough to slip into, but ended at the
tent wall. Exhausted, Agouhanna had to stop
working.

He stretched himself out on the bed of pine
boughs and rested for a long while. Then he
went back to work. The hole was getting larger,
and now was reaching to the outside of the tent.
Fortunately the moonlight was shining on the
opposite side of the tent, leaving in darkness the

side where the child was working. Besides, before setting to work Agouhanna had memorized his bearings by observing the setting sun and the location of the tent with respect to the sun. His intelligent observations had stood him in good stead.

The decisive moment had come. If he were successful, the worst would be over. Agouhanna insinuated himself into the hole by sliding along on his back. He raised his head slowly outside the tent and looked in all directions. He saw no warriors. Everything was quiet. They had all gone to sleep, believing that they had pitched the tent and sealed it so solidly that the child would be unable to get out.

With infinite cautiousness, he slid completely outside and stood up—but not completely, in order that he might remain in the shadow of the tent. As he had foreseen, the moon made it as clear as day. The child saw every single detail around him. Nothing moved, nothing looked suspicious. The lake glistened. On the other side was his tent, which had sheltered him for so many long days. Once he got that far, he would already feel at home.

He took his bearings. He would start by plunging into the woods, and after he had gotten far enough away from the enemy warriors, he would head toward the lake to follow its turnings, keeping to the shore until he had reached his tent.

In accordance with his plan, he slipped noiselessly into the thick woods that were only a few steps away, then stopped in order to check on the tents and the area around them. Nothing. No motion, no sound. The warriors were surely asleep. He had not aroused their suspicion. If he could find his way back, he would be safe—and his people too, for he'd have a whole night's lead on the warriors. He was no longer afraid, and he felt very calm. Like a silent shadow, he plunged still deeper into the forest, then doubled back toward the lake.

Following the lakeshore from a distance, he easily found his way back to his little tent, which was still there. Agouhanna looked at it with joy. Should he take it apart? No, there was no time for that. Doubtless the enemy would see it if they wound around the lake, but what was more important was that he reach his people before the enemy did. Agouhanna knew the way from his tent to the village very well. He would surely be able to find it once again, even if the night made things more difficult to recognize.

Without losing a moment, he continued on his way. He ran, then stopped, then began to run once more. Night, in the forest, was filled with traps, but Agouhanna could not have cared less. He was no longer afraid, and the idea of calling upon the bear, his guardian, didn't even occur to him. He had one fixed idea in mind — to rejoin his people before the enemy, for the warriors might awaken at any moment, discover his flight, and immediately set off in pursuit.

Agouhanna ran like this for a long time. But he felt himself growing more and more tired. Suddenly he stumbled over a thick root and tumbled into a thicket. Exhausted, done in, Agouhanna could not get up again. He dropped off quickly into a deep sleep — it was so late, and he had come so far!

When he awoke, a ray of sunlight touched his eyes lightly. The birds were singing at the top of their voices. Agouhanna rubbed his eyes, and then asked himself where he might really be, and what he was doing there. He was stretched out on his back in some tall grass; his arms and legs ached. Little by little everything came back to him. He smiled. Now it was broad daylight and he was far from the enemy and close to his people, for he was very familiar with this corner of the forest which surrounded him.

Just a little farther on, and he would hear the sounds of the voices that he knew; he would see the high staked wall that surrounded his village, the sweet face of his mother, the fine, head-strong, beautiful features of Little Doe, the straightforward and strong head of White Eagle. Suddenly he was seized by a wild desire to see them again. Oddly enough, he didn't think of his father—even though, as a little boy who was afraid of everything, he had always had him on his mind.

Stirred by these thoughts and these desires, he was about to make the effort to get up when he heard some rather far-off cracking noises. The sounds were weak and irregular, but Agou-hanna had a very fine ear. The threat of enemy presence struck him like a slap in the face. Supposing it was the enemy? Maybe they had followed him, or picked up his tracks!

Another thing was even more strange. At this moment, Agouhanna was afraid—not for himself, but for his people. He didn't think of himself for a moment; but he could not bear the idea that they should be able to attack his village by surprise before he had the time to warn them.

Yet, would they dare, in broad daylight, to attack an enemy living in an area that was unfa-miliar to them? Agouhanna doubted it. But there he was. No doubt they wouldn't attack before nightfall, but if they were to discover him, he'd be done for! The cracking sounds were coming toward him. This time, Agouhanna's heart was pounding madly.

He called up his guardian with his whole soul, and after a moment, it seemed to him that he heard a sort of groaning not far from him. Reassured, he did not think of taking flight; he would certainly have been lost if the noises were coming from enemy warriors. He did not stir. This way, if they didn't bump into him on their path, he would be saved once again!

Suddenly he saw two of the warriors pass by, not far from him. Agouhanna held his breath. Two scouts, no doubt. The rest had to be quite far behind, very cautious, and ready to retreat at the slightest signal. The two warriors passed without seeing him. From the way that they were behaving, Agouhanna could figure out what they were looking for. Surely they wanted to capture him before he could warn his people of their presence. They even had to be asking themselves if he hadn't already reached his village. That certainly was making them even more cautious, for if the village was waiting for them ...!

Agouhanna remained for a long time without moving. Then, hearing nothing, he began to

crawl softly on the ground, sliding noiselessly like an adder. After long hours, he could finally see the high dark wall of his village through the foliage. A clearing of about five hundred feet separated the wall from the forest, in order to force an enemy to show himself if ever he attacked.

Once he had arrived at the edge of the forest, with the high wall of his village rising up before him like a barrier, Agouhanna hesitated. He felt very moved—only a few steps from him there breathed his own people. And they didn't even know that he was there, near them. What were they doing at this moment? The sun had almost set; they had to be getting ready for dinner.

But he heard nothing, and saw nothing move in the observation tower that surmounted the wall. Supposing they had already been attacked? Agouhanna's throat tightened. But the child speedily pushed the thought aside, and concentrated on the means he could use to contact his people and get inside the village.

Agouhanna found nothing which could really distract the enemy's attention while he was crossing this bare and completely exposed area. Nevertheless he had to make up his mind. Night would fall rapidly and the enemy, who had to be hiding nearby, were doubtless only waiting for the propitious moment to attack.

Finally he hit upon a plan of action. He would suddenly burst out of the forest, run as fast as he could up to the great gate of the stockade and then, once he was at the foot of the gate, he would begin to shout loudly to attract the attention of the people inside the fortress.

It was a dangerous risk to take, but what else could he do? For, if the enemy saw him, they would lead him back to the forest in order to murder him there, under cover. And if his people didn't hear his cries? Then it would be too late, and the young Iroquois would no longer be able to fall back.

But Agouhanna didn't want to hesitate any longer over these thoughts. He simply had to save his village from any possible attack. Agouhanna was so overwrought that, without even thinking of his guardian, without hesitating any more because of the possible dangers which might make his move a fatal one, he darted out toward the wall.

Now it made no difference who could see him running and bounding like a doe over dead trees and boulders. In this way he reached the great gate of the fortress. At the same instant, he cried out with all his might.

An echo repeated his cries all around the fortress and far into the forest. The child had taken a great risk—supposing the village was off on an expedition? Suppose there was no one inside? Having heard him and spotted him, the enemy would make quick work of him!

Suddenly Agouhanna heard a whistling. An arrow grazed his hair and slammed into the gate. So the enemy had already seen him, and since they had no time to take him back into the forest, they were trying to kill him on the spot. Without even thinking about being afraid, Agouhanna began to call out again even while he flung himself to the ground in order to offer as small a target as possible to the enemy. How well he did it! Two other arrows arrived, planting themselves in the gate only a few inches above him.

All of a sudden the great gate was opened, and strong arms seized the boy and pulled him inside. Then the great gate closed once again. The young Iroquois had fainted.

When he regained consciousness, Agouhanna saw that he was lying in his parents' cabin. His mother, squatting at his side, gave him a beautiful smile when she saw his eyes open. Agouhanna tried to move, but his entire body ached.

His mother helped him to lift himself up, and sit on his bed of pine boughs covered with the same bearskin that he loved so much. Once he was sitting up, Agouhanna was able to smile at his mother, and to look all about him. How many familiar things he saw! But his father was not there. Agouhanna was disturbed by this.

His mother told him that his father was on the ramparts, defending the village with the other warriors, for the enemy had attacked as soon as Agouhanna had been pulled in. Their plan had doubtless been to attack the village during the night, but Agouhanna's intervention and his cries of alarm had forced them to decide to try to take the village by surprise, striking at once in the hope that the village's occupants would be unprepared to defend themselves.

But at the moment when Agouhanna's warning cries had penetrated the wall, the warriors on the inside were getting their bows and arrows ready for a hunt that was to take place the next day. Hearing the child's cries, they ran swiftly toward the wall and the great gate. While some were opening the gate and pulling Agouhanna inside, others were climbing up the walls. Within a short time, they were riddling with arrows the fifty-odd enemy warriors who were shooting flaming arrows at the walls of the fortress, and at the interior.

Very soon, a fire caught in a corner of the wall. Led by the cries of the defenders, the women brought buckets of water that the warriors threw on the fire, and succeeded in putting it out. Then fires started up in other areas that the women and the warriors extinguished in turn. The enemy, taking advantage of the fact that the defenders were occupied with putting out the flames, scaled the walls at various places on some hazardous ladders hastily made from tree limbs.

But the defenders welcomed them with tomahawk blows. Some of the enemy collapsed at the foot of the wall, killed by the tomahawks, while others fell somewhat farther off, under the arrows raining upon them from the fortress.

Afraid that they would be taken prisoner and tortured, all the others fled to the forest at the moment when the defenders, on orders from the old commander, were opening the great gate for a hand-to-hand combat with the enemy.

The defenders did not pursue the enemy into the forest, for the latter were surely hiding to surprise them. They came back inside the fortress and closed the great gate.

For three days and three nights the warriors of the village kept close surveillance all around the fort in order to avoid another surprise attack. But there was no trace of the enemy.

The firm defense of the fortress and the loss of a number of their men had served to discourage them. They were not to be seen again.

✷

Since Agouhanna had not been honored since the return of his comrades, and since he had saved the village from certain massacre, a great festival was organized solely for him, now that he had proved to be a real hero.

During the festival, the village celebrated his courage. White Eagle, along with the other boys, regarded his friend with great admiration. Even Owl, in spite of the feelings that he had harbored concerning Agouhanna, couldn't prevent himself from showing a certain admiration for the son of the old chieftain.

At a given moment, Agouhanna's father took a crown of vividly colored feathers, placed it on his son's head, and said to him in a voice loud enough to be heard by the entire assemblage, "My son, during your long fast you have seen a bear in your dreams, but you shall keep the name of Agouhanna, for it signifies 'a brave among the braves.' You have shown yourself to be courageous, and now you are truly my son.

In addition, I am naming you as my successor, and you shall be chieftain and commander of this village when I become too old to govern my people."

Then, turning toward the group of boys, he gave a signal to White Eagle and to Owl to step forward. When they stood before him, he said to them, "My son, Agouhanna, shall be at the head of my people. You, White Eagle, shall be his right arm and you, Owl, shall be his left arm. Both of you will obey my son, and later on you, too, will become renowned and respected commanders. You will faithfully guard my son and his people."

After that he addressed himself to Agouhanna: "My son, if you have a wish, let me hear it."

Even though Little Doe loved Agouhanna tenderly, in order to show her independence she had not wanted to take part in the celebration. She had character, that little one!

Agouhanna had been grieved by this. Without the presence of the little girl, something indispensable was missing from this festival. He saw now how much he depended on her. And at this moment he made a serious decision. He said to his father, "Yes, Father, I do want to express one desire: I want to marry Little Doe. If you agree to this, let them go seek her out.

And if it is your wish as well as mine, I beseech you to marry us."

The old chieftain displayed no surprise at these words. He ordered on the spot that Little Doe be sought out. When at last she arrived before the chieftain, he gently took the little girl's right hand and said to her, "Agouhanna, my son, desires you as his wife. What is your wish?"

"I want to be Agouhanna's wife," Little Doe said quickly and firmly, but with her eyes lowered. The old chieftain took his son's hand, united it with Little Doe's, and in a loud voice uttered these words: "You are now husband and wife. When I shall have decided upon it, you will live together and establish a home."

The entire assemblage began to sing hymns of joy and to dance around the great fire, pulling the young couple into the circle with them.

Thus Agouhanna had become so brave that, by marrying Little Doe, he didn't even hear the familiar growling of the bear.

AUTHOR

CLAUDE AUBRY was born in Morin Heights, a small village in the Laurentian Mountains in Canada, on October 23, 1914. When he was a boy, he had to walk two miles through fields and woods to school. He received a B.A. from the University of Montreal and a B.L.S. from McGill University. Two of his children's books, *The King of the Thousand Islands* and *The Christmas Wolf,* won the Bronze Medal (the Canadian version of the Newbery Medal). He is the author of, among other works, *The Magic Fiddler and Other Legends of French Canada.* He lives in Ottawa, where he is director of the Ottawa Public Library and of the Eastern Ontario Regional Library System.

ILLUSTRATOR

JULIE BRINCKLOE, a native of Mare Island, California, studied art at Sweet Briar College and Carnegie Mellon University. Although she has written and illustrated several children's stories, AGOUHANNA is her first illustrated book to be published. Miss Brinckloe is now a resident of New York City.

PaperJacks

FLINT AND FEATHER:
The Complete Poems of
E. Pauline Johnson
Introduction by
Theodore Watts-Dunton

Pauline Johnson was a Mohawk
Indian born on the Six Nations
Reserve near Brantford, Ontario, in
1862. In her poetry she expressed, as
no one had done before, the intensity
and passion, the hopes and feelings –
and much, too, of the tragedy – of her
people. The easy, flowing movement
of her lines suggests rippling waters,
tribal music, the rhythmic lift of the
paddle. You will want to read her
poems aloud, and often. $1.25

PaperJacks

THE INCREDIBLE JOURNEY
by Sheila Burnford

Immortalized by Walt Disney, this is the world-famous story of three animals who found their way home through the wooded wilderness of Ontario. There was Luath, a young and gentle Labrador with a red-gold coat and a noble head. There was Tao, the hunter, a sleek wheat-coloured Siamese cat. And there was Bodger, an old, half-blind Bull Terrier. This unlikely trio walked and ran, fought and struggled together against overwhelming odds, escaped death at almost every step, and finally reached home, to end their incredible journey. *Illustrated.* $1.25

PaperJacks

HOCKEY:
Tips on Playing Better Hockey
Tips on Understanding Hockey
by Scott Meyers

Do you know which plays keep
defencemen awake at night, and give
goalies nightmares? Are you confused
by referees' signals? Do your drop
passes embarrass your team, and you?
Do you know why goalies slide back
and forth across the goal mouth at the
beginning of each period? Have you
ever wondered how the super-stars
relax in the dressing room? Here is a
book to answer these questions and
hundreds more, with clear explana-
tions of the game and illustrated tips
for minor league players anxious to
improve their skill. $.95